Mother Night

By Denys Cazet

Hooked On Phonics®

First published in 1989 by Orchard Books, A Division of Franklin Watts, Inc.
This edition published in 1998 by Gateway Learning Corporation.

ISBN 1-887942-49-1

Mother Fox whispers, "Sweet dreams."

Mother Night is here

to hush the earth,

to shake her dark quilt,

The mice dream.

The foxes dream.

The bears dream.

The ravens dream.

The earth is hushed.

The stars are fading east to west, and then, edged in dawn,

Mother Night is gone. Now who will wake her children?

Mother Fox.

She will wake her children, singing them a song.

He will wake his children and tell them a new-day story.

Mother Raven.

as it fills the world.